Lily's Driftwood Bay

The Snowy Delivery

Let's find sea treasure!

centum

LILY'S DRIFTWOOD BAY: THE SNOWY DELIVERY

A CENTUM BOOK 978-1-910917-10-7

Published in Great Britain by Centum Books Ltd

Centum Books Ltd, 20 Devon Square,

Newton Abbot, Devon, TQ12 2HR, UK

books@centumbooksltd.co.uk

CENTUM BOOKS Limited Reg. No. 07641486

This edition published 2016

A CIP catalogue record for this book is available

from the British Library.

Printed in China

1 3 5 7 9 10 8 6 4 2

Hello! I'm Lily.
I live in a beach hut by the sea
with my Dad and my best friend, Gull.
Inside our hut is my telescope - it's
very useful for spotting sea treasures
that wash up on the beach.
When Gull and I find some sea treasure,
it always starts a fun adventure
across the way... on Driftwood Bay!
Are you ready to come with us today?

It's very cold today, so I'm helping Dad to collect sticks for the fire.
The fire will heat our beach hut and keep us nice and warm.

"Put all the sticks you find in the basket," Dad tells me.
"But remember, they must be dry or they won't burn."

"Okay, Dad," I say.

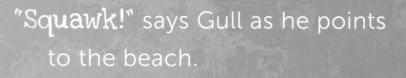

"Squawk!" says Gull as he points
to the beach.

"Sea treasure! I'm going to see what it is, Dad. Okay?"

"Okay, Lily! I'll be here making the fire if you need me,"

says Dad, smiling!

Down by the sea, we find some treasure washed ashore!

"Look Gull, it's a woolly hat! But who could it belong to?

Maybe it's a sailor's hat... Maybe it's a fisherman's hat...
or maybe it's a snowman's hat...

...from across the way
on Driftwood Bay..."

"All aboard for Driftwood Bay!" comes a familiar voice.
It's Salty in Delilah, his trusty boat.

"Coming aboard Captain Salty!" I shout to him.
"Squawk!" says Gull.

"Welcome aboard, shipmates!" Salty smiles,
as he fits my life jacket.

We're off to Driftwood Bay!

"Oooh, look Gull. It's Snowing!" I point excitedly. Driftwood Bay is covered in snow.

"Brrrrr! Blisterin, barnacles! It's been snowing for days now." Salty tells me.

"Look what I found, Salty!" I show him the woolly hat.
"Is it yours?"

"Heh, heh, no young Lily. It's not mine. I've got my trusty Captain's hat to keep my head warm," Salty says.
"It looks like a hat that might belong to Hatsie. She does love a good hat!"

"And she'll need it in this chilly weather," I say.
"Let's find her!"

"Land Ho!" cries Salty as we approach the jetty.

"Thanks Salty. We're off to find Hatsie."

"I'll come with you shipmates" says Salty.
"You might need some help finding her
in all this snow."

And off we go!

9

When we get to Hatsie's henhouse she's not at home —
but her Clickety Clackety Train is.

"It's too snowy to drive the train today," I say.
"I wonder where she could be?"

"She'll be off delivering the post like she
always does - a little bit of snow won't
stop Hatsie," says Salty.

"Squawk!" says Gull. He's spotted some footprints in the snow!

"Why," says Salty. "These look like hen-shaped footprints to me."

"Let's follow them!" I say.

"Okay, Lily," Salty smiles.

Off we go through the snow following Hatsie's tracks.
We wonder where they will lead first.

It's not long before we find out!

"Hello, Wee Rabbit!" says Salty. The footprints stop at Wee
Rabbit's Treehouse. "Have you seen Hatsie today?"

"Yes I have," replies Wee Rabbit, taking us inside.
"She's delivering all of the parcels by foot today
because of all the snow."

"That's my Hatsie," says Salty. "She wouldn't let a little bit of snow get in the way."

"Hatsie's on her way to the Cockle Café, with a very big parcel for Nonna," Wee Rabbit tells us. "Something for the snow..!"

"Ooh, let's go to see Nonna!" I say to Salty and Gull.

As we say goodbye to Wee Rabbit, we find more hen prints in the snow. We're on the right path!

As we pass by the pond we see Bull looking a bit puzzled.

"Where has all the water gone, Lily?"
Bulls asks sadly.

"Oh Bull!" I smile, "The water has frozen and turned to ice."

"Oh goody! Why don't we do some ice-skating then?"

"Ho, ho, I think I'll stand by and watch,"
says Salty. "I prefer my water wet
and wavy!"

"Squawk!" Gull laughs.

The pond makes a perfect ice-skating rink, but
because it's very small, and Bull is very big, we
keep bumping into each other!

15

"Phew! All this skating has made me hungry," says Bull.

"We're off to the Cockle Café to find Hatsie. Why don't you come with us?"

"Great idea!" smiles Bull.

Off we walk through the snow – Salty, Bull, myself and Gull, but soon it becomes very deep.

"Jump on my back and I'll give you a ride, Lily," Bull says.

Riding through the snow on Bull's back is lots of fun!

When we eventually arrive at the Cockle Café we find Nonna and a very tired and cold Hatsie. She's warming up with a cup of Nonna's Barnacle Broth.

"Goodness me. What a busy day for deliveries. And what a very big, heavy parcel that was, Nonna!"

"Oh thank you so much, Hatsie," says Nonna. "It's a new sledge! Now we're all set for the Winter Games!"

"Winter Games?" cries Bull excitedly. "What's that then?"

"Well dear, at the Winter Games we have lots of frosty fun outside, then come inside afterwards for hot Barnacle Broth and freshly baked Puffin Muffins!"

"Oh! That sounds great," says Bull, his tummy rumbling. "Especially the Puffin Muffins part."

In all the excitement I almost forget about the hat! I give it to Hatsie.

"Th-h-h-ank y-ou-ou, Lily," says Hatsie, still shivering as I put the hat on her head. "But it's not mine."

The hat is way too big for Hatsie!

"I can't see a thing!" she giggles as it flops down over her face.

"Hold on, Hatsie!" I say. I have an idea and ask Nonna to help me.

With a snip-snip here, and a snip-snip there, we've soon turned the hat into something new.

"Ta-da!" I say to Hatsie. "We've made you a brand new snow cloak to keep you warm on your winter deliveries!"

"Oh how wonderful, Lily!" says Hatsie. "Thank you."

"Give us a twirl!" says Salty.

"Ooh, can I have one of those?" asks Bull.

"I think we would need a very big hat," says Nonna laughing.

21

Lord Stag, Wee Rabbit, Puffin and The Squeaky Mice arrive and we all go outside for the Winter Games!

"First event is Snowman building!" announces Nonna.

Bull and I team up. Bull is great at rolling the snow to make the snowman's head and body.

The Squeaky Mice make three little snow mice.

Hatsie's snowman looks just like her.

Salty's snowman has a pirate eyepatch. Ooo-arrrgh!

Then Nonna leads us to the top of a hill for the sledge race.

"On your marks, get set, go!" shouts Nonna.

"Wee-heeeeeeeeeee!" says Wee Rabbit.

Salty zooms ahead and wins the race.

Soon, everyone is exhausted – and we all go into the Cockle Café for Nonna's delicious hot food and to warm up by the fire.

"This was the best day ever," says Bull. "Thanks for all the yummy food, Nonna!"

"Thank you Hatsie for delivering the sledge," says Nonna.

"And thank you Lily for my new snow cloak!" says Hatsie.

Everyone agrees! It was a great day on **Driftwood Bay**.

"Lily...!" calls Dad.
"It's time to go home now."

Back at the beach hut, the fire is lit. It's lovely and cosy.

"Look outside, Lily," says Dad...

Beautiful white fluffy flakes. "It's snowing!" I shout. "Hooray!"

It's been a wonderful day and now tomorrow will be another fun snowy day too!

Read It Again Activities!

Can you answer these questions now you have read the story? If you are not sure, then read the story again.

1 What was Lily helping her Dad collect to make a fire?

2 Which friend did Lily ice skate with?

3 What did Lily use to make Hatsie's snow cloak?

4 Who won the sledge race?

5 Why was Lily happy at the end?

Lots to Spot!

Check your answers on page 32!

Read the story again and shout out when you spot the things below.

Teapot

Snowball

Puffin Muffin

Rocking Horse

Sledge

Hatsie's Tracks

Snowy Fun!

Make your own fun on a cold snowy day with...

Yummy Snacks

Ask a grown-up to help you make hot chocolate, sizzling sausages and warm toast to help warm you up when it's cold outside.

Snowy art

Collect sticks, stones and your own treasures to make a picture or decorate a snowman.

Lily's tip:

If you are playing outside, make sure you wrap up warm and always wear a hat, scarf and gloves.

Snowy shaker

Create some snowy fun with Lily's snow shaker.

What you need :

- An old jar
- Scissors
- Picture or photo
- Glue
- Water
- Glitter

1. Wash out your jar and let it dry.

2. Take your picture and make sure it fits your jar. If not use scissors to trim the picture to size.

3. Using glue, stick your photo or picture to the outside of the jar and let it dry.

4. Fill your jar with some water nearly to the top.

5. Now add lots of glitter to the water in the jar.

6. Screw on your lid tightly, then shake your jar and watch the snow flurry.

Lily's tip:

Make sure your lid is screwed on tight before you start to shake!

Lily's tip:

If you like, you could stick a plastic toy to the inside of the jar lid instead of sticking a picture on the outside.

Answers!

Read It Again Activities!

1 Lily was collecting wood.

2 Lily went ice skating with Bull.

3 The woolly hat sea treasure.

4 Salty won the sledge race.

5 Lily was happy because it was snowing.

Lots To Spot!

The teapot is on page 17.

The snowball is on page 22.

The Puffin Muffin is on page 25.

The rocking horse is on page 13.

The sledge is on page 23.

Hatsie's tracks are on page 10.